PIG'S

Season's Finale

Barbara Catchpole

Illustrated by Dynamo

Ransom

Finale

First of all, you say it 'fin-ah-lee'.

You knew that? Oh well, I didn't know. When Raj told me, I felt a right muppet.

I love those episodes on 'Grey's Anatomy' or 'CSI' when it's the last one in the series. That's what they call the finale.

Like when a plane crashes onto the hospital while there's a flood and a gunman on the loose and a pretty girl is having a baby stuck in the lift. The actors have gallons of blood all over

5

their uniforms. (Mum says it's tomato sauce.)

Then there's an earthquake
or a giant wave (there's
another funny
word for it, but
I forget what it
is) and the roof
caves in.

It's called a
tsunami, Pig.

Mum says they do it to make you watch the next series. And to kill off all the actors who have found a better job or have had a row with someone.

Like if there's a really stroppy actor nobody likes. Or if there's a really old actor who needs a rest, they put him on life support for a few episodes.

Anyway, nobody dies during my story, not even Auntie Patsy or an alligator. So, chill!

Just a bit about Mum

Does your Mum get stressy? Mine does!

I don't really get it. Just small things set her off. Like a gas bill. Or the way that Suki leaves the bath full of slippery smelly pink stuff. Or Gran phoning Mum up to ask if she has a bikini Gran can borrow.

Or Gran phoning her up at all.

She went spare when I got black paint down the back of my purple sweatshirt in Art (I bet it was Zac who did it).

I don't get it – Mum has a lovely family and she doesn't have a lot to do.

She says she needs 'time to herself'. What on Earth does that mean?

Last Saturday

Mum sat down on the sofa in her ratty old pink pyjamas that used to be red before the washing machine went wrong.

In one hand she had a cup of tea and in the other a huge piece of coffee cake (at least a third of a big cake).

I'm just saying. I'm not allowed all that.

Vampire Baby was having a stay-up-and-shout over at Gran's (he doesn't sleep at night at all).

Gran wanted Vampire Baby because she'd had a row with the woman in the flat next door and she wanted to keep her up all night.

Don't cross my gran! Don't make her angry!

You wouldn't like her when she's angry.

(Vampire Baby is like a secret weapon. We should rent him out at night, or sell him to the army or something. He could make any enemy surrender after just one night.)

Mum said:

'Today is my day off. I'm going to do nothing.'

My English teacher gave us a poem by some Scots bloke that was about how the best plans of mice and men get stuffed up.

I don't know what plans mice have.

'I must remember about mousetraps.'

'I'll nip down to the kitchen later and see if there are any crumbs next to the bread bin.'

'Think I'll have another ten or so babies next week.'

'Today I'll leave little poos everywhere.'

'I must eat any homework that's been left out.'

I know about men's plans though.

My dad used to spend ages planning what horses to back, while I was waiting to go and play football down the rec. He knew loads about it. It was strange he didn't win very often.

He spent ages planning Uncle Nick's stag night as well. I don't think that went very well either, because Uncle Nick never turned up for the wedding. They found him tied to a lamp post in the shopping centre.

13

We still had a good party though. The cake was lovely and there was lots of it because the bride's family went home.

I suppose some of Dad's plans must have worked out OK – OK for him, anyway.

I think Uncle Nick's still not talking to him.

Mice and men may be rotten planners, but Mum's plans were doomed. This is what happened in my 'series finale'.

The best laid plans of hamsters and men

Harry should have been in his big fluffy hamster bed. He wasn't. He was lying on the bottom of the cage. He wasn't moving.

I shook the cage a bit. Nothing.

I poked him with a teaspoon. Nothing.

I tried to see if
his chest was going
up and down. Perhaps
we would have to
do artificial perspiration.

It's respiration,
not perspiration,
you muppet!

I looked at Mum, who was
just about to take a big bite of cake.

'Muuuum! Harry's ill!'

She put the cake down again and sighed.

She got up and dropped a bit of coffee cake in
the cage. Harry opened one eye but he didn't
move.

16

'They don't ...
well ... hamsters
are ... well ...
OK, we'll take him
down the vets, Pig.
Don't worry!'

Down the vets

Mum hates going down the vets! They charge so
much she says she might as well just stay at
home and burn money.

It was very noisy. Two big black dogs were
barking at each other.

'Bark, bark! Bark, bark!'

'Ralph!'

'Bark!'

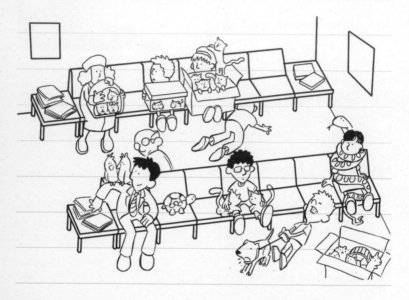

I got a bit stressy so I read all the posters
about fleas and ticks and worms and other
gross stuff.

A man in a dirty old mac came in with a

parrot with no feathers. He said it could sing a load of Spice Girls songs, but all it said was, 'Wanna banana, granddad?' over and over again.

Then a little boy had a ginger guinea pig that'd had its ear bitten off in a fight with another guinea pig. It kept going:

'Wee, wee, wee.'

(Not actually going for a wee - just making the noise. Harry was weeing a bit though. It was getting wet in the saucepan.)

We had to wait nearly an hour, but for the last ten minutes a mouse in a cage on the seat next

to me had twelve babies and I got to watch.
Mum said:

    'Glad I'm not a mouse! She won't get a

    moment to herself!'

We had put Harry
in a saucepan
because he eats
anything else (even
plastic). He was
moving about a bit
now, but he kept
dragging his foot after him.

He looked very sorry for himself. I was a bit
worried.

The vet was a very nice lady, even though she said a bad word when Harry bit her.

Turns out Mum took Harry's wheel out of his cage last night to clean it. He must have jumped on the wheel that wasn't there and hurt himself when he landed.

It's official: our hamster is an idiot.

The vet put a little lolly stick thing on his leg. It cost thirty quid and he ate it before we got home.

Mum said she could have bought six new

hamsters for thirty quid.

It did him good

though, because he

was running around

the saucepan like a

loony by the time

we tipped him out.

Mum sat back down on the sofa.

    'Ooff! My head hurts!'

She drank some cold tea and picked up the

coffee cake.

Suki

The phone went just as Mum was biting into the cake. She put it down again and sighed. It was Suki on her friend's phone.

I could hear Suki screaming and shouting.

Mum said:

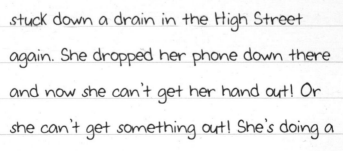

'Suki's got her hand stuck down a drain in the High Street again. She dropped her phone down there and now she can't get her hand out! Or she can't get something out! She's doing a lot of screaming. We'd better get down there! Could you calm her down while I get some butter?'

Well I tried, but Suki was crying and yelling.

I held the phone tight and told her not to sit down because dogs wee near drains. Oh, and I said that Mum said there weren't really alligators down there.

I asked her if she could hear any rats. I think I was helpful.

Suki's always getting bits of her stuck in things. So far she's got stuck in:

1. the fence that belongs to the bloke who won't give us our ball back at the back of the school field (that was to get a tennis ball)

2. the meerkat cage at the zoo (no idea)

3. the letter box at Tesco's (Mum's motor bike keys)

4.   Gran's biscuit jar, when she was four and
Dad said she wouldn't let go of the biscuits.
He had to break the jar with a hammer
and Gran was mad at him and made him
buy her a new jar and a packet of
Garibaldis.

Down the High Street

There was a big crowd around Suki. Mum had
brought the butter because that was how she
usually got Suki's hand out of things.

Suki didn't have her hand stuck down the drain.
Most of her was stuck down there. Only her top
half was showing.

She had dropped her mobile phone down the drain and the bloke from the Spare Gold Shop had got the cover off for her. She'd leaned right in, but she couldn't reach it. (It would have been great if she had fallen in head first!)

Suki had put her legs down and tried to pick her

phone up with her toes. She's really thin, but she got stuck.

Her best friend Beyonce (not the real one – this one's very round and lives near 'The Slug and Lettuce') was taking pictures with her phone.

Suki was screaming at the top of her lungs:

'Wahh! Get me out! I can't breathe!'

Well, she could breathe, obviously, because she was yelling. But Mum told her to breathe right out and to shut up yelling:

> 'No, breathe right out and if you don't shut up I won't help you, and breathe right out, you stupid girl.'

Mum tried to get some butter down between Suki and the drain. A nice crowd had gathered around and they were all yelling advice:

> 'You need cooking oil!'

> 'Make me a sandwich while you're there!'

'You need a saw! Cut her in half!'

'Mind the alligators!'

Mum got Suki under her arms and pulled. The crowd yelled:

'Heave – one, two, three, – heave!'

Suki didn't move, but the butter made her slippery and Mum slid off her and sat down in the road with a thump.

That was when the man from the Spare Gold Shop called the fire brigade.

The sirens got louder and louder. Mum sat in the road and held her head in her hands.

You should have been there

It was totally wicked! There were ten firemen and a proper fire engine and loads of police. They even closed the street

There were flashing lights everywhere and people talking on radios and saying TV stuff like:

'Over, over!'

and

'Victor, bravo!'

The bloke from the sweet shop gave me a bag of cola bottles, just because I was her brother.

I thought:

'This is what being famous is like.'

The police were saying:

'Move along, move along, nothing to see here,'

just like on TV. But there was loads to see – my nutcase sister for a start. You can see the whole thing on YouTube now, because Beyonce filmed it. You can just see the back of my head.

Two huge firemen got hold of Suki under her arms and a police lady put more goo on her and they pulled.

There was a loud squelchy noise like that sound jelly makes when you suck it out of the bowl, and suddenly Suki was out.

She was covered in butter and goo and

bad-smelling black muck
from down the drain.
Her face was covered in
black streaks of eye
make up. She only had
one eyelash and only one
of her huge earrings.
She really, really, stank.

She looked like a swamp
monster.

Looking at the huge firemen, she said:

'Cheers, guys! Why don't you all come back
to our house for some tea?'

Mum sighed again and rubbed her bottom where she had sat down suddenly in the road.

Fireman Sam

Mum got sausage and chips for ten firemen, four policemen, one police lady, me, Bob, Beyonce (she can eat loads so she counts as two), Raj, the man from the Spare Gold Shop and Suki (once she had been in the shower, phewee!).

Mum even fed Harry, although he was probably full up with lolly stick.

Suki was all clean and shiny and sitting eating a huge pile of sausage and chips. (Suki's so skinny — where do all those chips go? Is Suki bigger on the inside than the outside, like the Tardis?)

One of the firemen came and sat next to her
(he had to push a policeman off his chair first).

It was so crowded in the kitchen, you had to
push someone just to move.

He said:

'My name is Sam.'

Fireman Sam! He
looked a bit like
him too – big chin,
stary eyes and a
sticky-out nose.

He said:

'I was thinking ... '

I was surprised – he looked a bit dim. Still, he
did say he was thinking, so you had to believe
him.

' ... would you go out with me?'

Ha! I was right – he was a bit dim!

  'Oh yes,'

Suki said, *stuffing her mouth full of chips.*

Mum said:

  'Suki Kylie Green. Kim is your boyfriend.

He's teaching you to drive!'

'Yeah, I forgot! Have you got a car, Sam?'

'Yes!'

'That's OK then, Mum. I'll just text Kim
and tell him he's dumped!'

'But ... but ... '

Mum sat on the sofa and Raj brought her a cup of tea and a piece of coffee cake. She was just biting into it when Kim came rushing in.

The fight

Kim and Sam were shouting at each other in the hall. Fireman Sam is huge and he blocked out all the light, so we couldn't see Kim.

Kim is very short and looks like Justin Bieber. So it was Fireman Sam versus Justin Bieber. Just like a weird nightmare WWF match!

'She's MY girlfriend!'

'Does she know that? I don't think so!'

'Get out of my way, you lout!'

'Push off, Titch!'

'Do you want
to fight?'

'Do YOU want
to fight?'

'I do if you do!'

'Come on, then!'

Suki started shouting.

'Don't fight – oh, don't fight!'

She wanted them to fight, though. She's mean!

Mum yelled:

'Stop them, Bob!'

It was just like Eastenders! Just like a row in
the Queen Vic!

'What can I do?'

Bob looked like he was going to cry. Gran says he

44

couldn't knock the skin off a rice pudding. All the

police went on eating chips.

Mum went out the back, ran round the end of

our road, let herself in

the front and yelled at

the top of her voice:

    'Pack it in!'

She brought them into the kitchen to 'talk

about it', but Kim just stood staring while Sam

fed Suki chips.

It was like Sam was pushing chips into the

Tardis.

Mum pushed the police lady off the sofa. She
sat down, picked up her cake, opened her mouth,
put the slice in and ...

... Santa came rushing in the back door.

'Gran's been

arrested!'

Mum sighed and put the cake down.

Gran is arrested in Cheapomart

Gran had been skateboarding in Cheapomart.

Trying to do a double pivot, she lost control and went flying into a display of high-viz jackets from Russia that were cheap that week. One of them wrapped round her head and she couldn't see, so she knocked over a big wall of toilet rolls and ended up in the freezer. With her legs in the air.

It would have been OK, but she lost her teeth in the freezer. So when they tried to pull her out, she tried to get back in.

She tried to tell them, but she couldn't because she didn't have any teeth. She just mumbled at them and waved her arms about.

The police thought she was bonkers (they're not far wrong). Mum says she's mad as two balloons.

Mum yelled:

'What about Vampire Baby?'

Santa said:

'What baby? Oh, I think she took him with
her. I wonder where he is ... '

I'll tell you what happened

I'll tell you because it's pants when you have to
wait to find out. On telly, by the time you
watch the next episode, you've forgotten what
happened the last time because it was six
months ago.

So this is what happened:

1. They found Vampire Baby in his buggy, next

to the baked beans, sound asleep.

2. Suki is going out with Fireman Sam. Kim
   was gutted. If you ask me, it's a lucky
   escape! A fire escape!

3. Harry is much better, thank you for asking.

4. They found Gran's teeth in a tub of ice
   cream (Chunky Monkey). They let her keep
   the tub.

   The police gave her a 'caution', which is like
   when a teacher tells you not to do it again.
   And Mum told her she was 'a mad old bat'.

They had a bit of a row, but I think they've made it up now.

5. I ate the coffee cake – all of it – and felt a bit sick.

6. Bob had the cold tea. He asked Mum: 'Have you had a nice rest today, Susan?'

and she emptied the tea over his head.

Now she's having some more 'time to herself'.

See you soon!

How many **PIG** books have you read?

About the author

Barbara Catchpole was a teacher for thirty years and enjoyed every minute. She has three sons of her own who were always perfectly behaved and never gave her a second of worry.

Barbara also tells lies.